That
Crazy
Eddie
and the
Science
Project
of Doom

That Crazy Eddie

and the Science Project of Doom

by Judy Cox

illustrated by Blanche Sims

SCHOLASTIC INC.

New York Toronto London Auckland Sydney
Mexico City New Delhi Hong Kong Buenos Aires

ISBN-13: 978-0-439-02800-4
ISBN-10: 0-439-02800-0

12 11 10 9 8 7 6 5   8 9 10 11 12/0

Printed in the U.S.A.   40

First Scholastic printing, May 2007

To Chris
and the boys of Cub Scout Den 3.
Didn't we have fun!

v

Contents

Chapter One
Fifty Dollars!

Matt saw the poster on the second Friday of October. It was hanging on the wall outside Mrs. Gonzales's third-grade classroom.

THIRD-GRADE SCIENCE FAIR!
First Place Prize: Fifty-Dollar Gift Certificate
Open to teams of two or more

Matt didn't bother to read the rest of the rules. He just kept seeing two words, over and over, as if they glowed: FIFTY DOLLARS.

Fifty dollars was the exact amount he needed to buy the skateboard of his dreams. The one at Big-Mart. The one with neon flames and glow-in-the-dark skulls.

He had to find Eddie and tell him. The poster said teams of two or more could enter. That would be us, thought Matt. Matt and Eddie! The best team of all.

Matt hurried down the hall to the school cafeteria. He clutched his brown lunch sack in his hand. Noisy first graders pushed past him on their way to lunch.

Matt could see yellow maple trees through the hall windows. Large paper pumpkins decorated the walls. Fall! His favorite season.

He pushed open the cafeteria doors and paused for a minute in the doorway. The noise washed over him. What a great sound!

He might be the only kid in the world who was glad summer vacation was over.

Summers were boring. No Eddie. As soon as school was out, Eddie went to live with his dad in Portland. He didn't come back until Labor Day.

School was cool. Eddie and more Eddie, every single day!

Eddie slid into the seat beside Matt. He dropped his tray on the table with a bang.

Eddie wore a knit cap pulled low over his ears. His skinny neck stuck up out of his sweatshirt. Matt thought he looked a little bit like a turtle—if turtles wore glasses.

"Did you see the science fair poster?" Matt asked. "If we win, I can buy a skateboard like yours!"

Eddie grinned. "Gosh, my dad would be proud if we won! Science is his favorite thing. He's a geologist, you know. In Portland."

Eddie's eyes looked suddenly big behind his glasses. Matt knew how much Eddie missed his dad.

Then Eddie grinned his big old Eddie grin. "Listen, I have a great idea for a project! Something my dad showed me!"

"Yeah? What?" Matt couldn't wait to hear Eddie's idea.

"Are you talking about the science fair?" Allison set her tray down and sat across from Matt. Allison was in Mrs. Gonzales's class, too. Allison reminded Matt of the snooty cat in the cat food ad. The one who turned up her nose at the food.

"We're going to win," said Matt. "Eddie is the king of crazy ideas! And he has a brilliant idea for winning the science fair. Right, Eddie?"

Eddie nodded. He couldn't talk because he had stuffed a whole hard-boiled egg into his mouth.

Brittany slammed her tray down next to Allison. "Win? You guys? No way," she said. "Victor and I are going to win."

Victor slid his lunch tray next to Brittany's and grinned. "Yep," he said. "I can see that fifty dollars now." He rubbed his fingers together as if he were rubbing dollar bills. "Cold hard cash!"

"Only greedy pigs care about the money," said Allison. "But Mrs. Gonzales said anybody who enters will get fifty points of extra credit."

Allison flipped her hair over her shoulder. "And that would guarantee me an A+!"

Matt frowned. Everybody knew Allison was a brain. What chance would he and Eddie have with Allison in the fair?

"But you have to have a partner, don't you?" said Eddie. "'Teams of two or more,' right? So you can't enter."

"Jasmine will be my partner, right, Jasmine?" Allison turned to the black-haired girl who had just sat down. Jasmine nodded but didn't answer. Jasmine was shy. She never said much.

Matt groaned. The only thing worse than a brain like Allison was another brain like Jasmine. Now they were really in trouble.

He sighed and shook his head. He opened his paper sack. He pulled out the neatly wrapped items. He set everything out in a row. He liked to inspect his food before eating.

Bologna sandwich with pickles. Good, his favorite. Carrot sticks. Two chocolate-chip cookies. Yum. A carton of chocolate milk. A napkin.

"Look at me, I'm the Monopoly guy!" said Eddie. He propped a dried apricot behind his glasses and squinted to hold it up.

"But what about the science fair?" Matt asked, unwrapping his sandwich. "We have to sign up today. What's your great idea?"

Eddie opened his eyes, and the apricot fell out. He took a bite.

"Listen," he said, chewing noisily. "I can't say with *certain people sitting right here*." He pointed at Allison, who made a face.

"You sign us up," Eddie continued. "Let me take care of the idea." He swallowed the apricot and reached for another egg.

Relieved, Matt bit into his sandwich. That Eddie! No matter what he had in mind, it was sure to be good.

Chapter Two

All Aboard
for Big-Mart

"All aboard!" yelled Dad. "This train leaves the station in six minutes!"

Matt bounded down the stairs. It was Saturday morning. Dad was going to Big-Mart. Matt and his brother Luke had begged to go, too.

Mom wasn't going. She hated Big-Mart. "Too many people!" she said. "Too much stuff! I'll just stay here and get caught up on my garden. I have a few more tulip bulbs I want to plant before the first frost."

But Matt loved Big-Mart. Shelves and shelves of stuff to buy! Where else could you get food, clothes, tools, and toys all in the same store?

Matt jumped into the car next to Dad. Dad wore jeans and a football sweatshirt. He ran his hand through his curly hair, making it stick up. He looked like Luke when he did that.

"Hey!" said Luke. "I was going to sit in front! I outrank you, squirt!" Luke was thirteen.

Matt didn't bother to reply. Luke knew the rules. The first kid downstairs got the front seat. Luke would just have to sit in back.

Luke climbed into the backseat. He bumped the back of Matt's seat. Matt ignored him. Luke put on his headphones and settled into silence.

They drove along the wet streets to the outskirts of town. Past fast-food places, car lots, and shopping malls. Matt could

see the big, blue-and-red Big-Mart sign up ahead. Now that the rain had stopped, the sign sparkled in the cold October sunshine.

Dad pulled into the Big-Mart parking lot. The lot was full of cars.

"All ashore that's going ashore!" said Dad. He opened the car door.

They crossed the lot to the store. The big, double glass doors parted with a *whoosh*. Matt grabbed a shopping cart.

The best part of Big-Mart was the

miles of concrete floors. The shopping cart skidded smoothly across the floor.

"Hey," said Luke. "Wouldn't it be cool to come in here at night and skateboard?"

Matt imagined zipping up and down the aisles. "Zoom! Whoosh! Whee!" He pushed the cart faster.

Dad walked up and down each aisle. He checked his list. Luke wandered off to look at magazines. Matt pushed the cart three steps. Then he stepped up. He glided a few yards, careful not to bump anyone.

Soon, Dad would tell him to cut it out. He always did. But until then, Matt would ride.

Dad threw a giant bag of kitty litter into the cart. He added two boxes of cat food.

Matt saw a tall display just past the pet food aisle. He grabbed Dad's elbow. "Look!" He pulled Dad over to show him.

Neon orange flames. Glow-in-the-dark skulls. The exact skateboard he would buy with the science fair prize money!

"So this is the one," said Dad. "Guess you better make a first-place science project."

"Hey, Matt!" Matt turned around to see two of his friends from Mrs. Gonzales's class.

"Are you guys talking about the science fair?" asked Michael Sanchez. "We have got the best idea ever. I got it out of a science fair book from the library."

"Wowie, zowie. That money is as good as mine." Michael Black's eyes shone with excitement.

"Ours," said Michael S., poking him with a pencil. "We're a team, remember?"

Michael B. smiled. "Yeah," he said. "Team First Place." He gave Michael S. a high five.

Michael B. waved at Matt. "See you in class!" he yelled. The two Michaels ran down the pet food aisle.

Now even the two Michaels were in the contest! What chance did he and Eddie have? He gave the skateboard one last look.

"Eddie won't tell me what his idea is," he told Dad. "He just gave me a list of the stuff to get. He's bringing the rest today."

Matt whisked the cart around the corner to the craft section. "Brown and green paint. Brushes," he said. He dropped paint and brushes into the cart.

Matt peered at the list. "Baking soda. Check. Vinegar. Check. Red food coloring. Check. Dishwashing liquid. Check. I wonder what Eddie wants us to do with all this."

Dad laughed and shook his head. "You and Eddie. Water and oil. Be careful, sport. Your friend Eddie is kind of a loose cannon, you know."

"What do you mean?" Matt was puzzled.

Dad ruffled Matt's hair. "Remember the time he started a fire in the front yard? He convinced you that it was a great idea. He even had you bringing him the matches! Luckily, the grass was too wet to burn."

"Oh, yeah," said Matt. "But that was years ago. He hasn't been in trouble since."

Dad shot him a look. "Seems to me that building a roller coaster out of his mom's laundry basket was just last spring."

Matt hid a grin. The laundry basket hadn't worked, but it had been fun. Until it broke. Mrs. Hampton wasn't too pleased, though.

Matt rolled the cart up to the checkout counter. Luke reappeared. He dropped a video game magazine into the cart.

Dad handed it back. "I'm not paying for that," said Dad. "Use your allowance."

Luke grinned. He fished his wallet out of his jeans. "Okay, okay. Can't blame a guy for trying."

Dad paid for the items. Matt pushed the cart through the parking lot. Three running steps and then glide. Luke jogged along next to him.

"Dibs on the front seat!" Luke yelled.

Matt scrambled into the back. He couldn't wait to see what Eddie had in mind! But would it be crazy enough to beat Allison?

Chapter Three

Yucko

On Saturday afternoon, Matt stood in his garage. The October sun blazed through the open garage doors behind him. But inside the dark garage, Matt saw only a big, blobby mess.

Eddie knelt on the garage floor, slapping on wet paper strips. He stood up and looked at Matt. "Well, what do you think?"

Mittens, Matt's cat, padded over. She sniffed at the wet mess. She put her ears back and hissed.

Matt narrowed his eyes. He agreed with Mittens. He shook his head. "One word," he told Eddie. "Yucko."

Eddie frowned. "It doesn't look that bad," he said. "I mean it won't, once we get it painted."

Matt prodded the gray pile of wet newspapers with his sneaker. "It doesn't look at all like a volcano," he complained. "How is this mess ever going to win first place?"

What a letdown. Eddie usually had great, crazy, wonderful ideas. And now, just when they needed a great, crazy, wonderful idea, all they got was wet paper.

Mittens pounced on a stray piece of newspaper. Matt scooted her out of the way with his foot.

"Listen!" said Eddie. "You know what? It just needs more gunk!"

He tore a strip of paper and soaked it in the flour-and-water mix in the plastic tub. He slapped the paper on the volcano. He smoothed it down with his fingers.

"See? Like that!" Eddie sat back on his heels. He grinned at Matt.

Matt folded his arms. He tilted his head. He squinted at the mess. First one side, then the other. He shook his head. Either way, it still looked like a mess.

"It's crooked," he said.

"You're crooked," said Eddie impatiently. "Look. After it dries, we'll paint it green and brown. With white for snow around the crater. It'll be great! Then we'll fill it with baking soda and vinegar. Dishwashing liquid. And red food coloring!"

Eddie waved his arms. "FIZZZZZT! There she blows! Hot lava oozing down the sides! Run for your life!"

Matt peered at the mound of gray, soggy paper. For a minute, he could almost see it the way Eddie described.

Then the picture dissolved. It was just

a wet, gray mass again. He sighed and shook his head.

"You know what your problem is?" asked Eddie. "You don't have any imagination."

"And you have too much," said Matt stubbornly.

"Well, somebody in this outfit has to." Eddie rolled some wet newspaper into a ball. He flipped it at Matt.

Mittens pounced on it. She batted it behind the car.

"Hey!" said Matt. He was still grouchy.

Eddie grinned. He flipped another ball of wet paper at Matt. It caught him on the chin. "Come on! Lighten up!"

Matt started to smile. That Eddie! He scooped up some paper pulp. He flung it at Eddie. The wet paper hit Eddie in the middle of his sweatshirt.

Eddie laughed. He pushed up his glasses. "This means war!" he yelled, filling both hands with newspaper pulp.

"No-o-o!" Matt hollered. He took cover behind the car. He laughed so hard his ribs ached. Mittens dashed outside.

Soon strings of soggy newspaper, flour, and water covered the floor. Water dripped down Matt's hair, dribbled down his nose, and splashed onto his shirt. He had to laugh when he looked at Eddie. The lenses of Eddie's glasses were papered over. Eddie peered over the top to see.

"What's going on?"

Matt turned around.

Mom stood in the doorway. Her hands were on her hips. A look of horror crossed her face. She wasn't looking at Matt. She wasn't looking at Eddie.

Matt turned to see.

Behind him, Mom's dark blue car dripped with gray streamers of wet paper. Flour-and-water mix trailed down in streaks of white, striping the car like a zebra.

"Uh-oh," said Eddie quietly.

"'Uh-oh' is right," said Mom. "Car wash time. Now. You've got to get it all off. Quickly, before it dries." She went to get her keys so she could back the car out of the garage onto the driveway.

As they sprayed the car with water, Eddie's eyes got a strange gleam. Matt knew that look. Eddie had an idea.

"Listen!" he said. "I know a way to make this volcano better than any volcano in the history of the world!"

"Oh, yeah? What?" Matt stopped soaping the car.

"That's for me to know and you to find out," Eddie said, closing his eyes.

"Come on, spill it. I'm your partner!"

"I'm going to do something better than that, I'm going to show you! But not yet. When the volcano is finished. Then, Shazzam! On the night of the fair, I'll work my magic and we'll be a shoo-in for first place!"

Matt felt a smile come to his face. First place! He could count on Eddie!

Eddie gave him a big Eddie grin. "I think *you* need a bath, too." And he turned the hose on Matt.

Chapter Four

In Bed with a Bug

On Sunday the volcano was dry enough to paint. Matt and Eddie worked on it until dinnertime. They set it on Dad's workbench to dry.

Even after Eddie went home, Matt kept checking on the volcano. It shone with fresh paint. Matt couldn't believe how good it looked. It was sure to win first place!

Luke came into the garage and stood beside Matt. "Hey, squirt," he said.

Mittens came in, too. She jumped up

on the workbench. She sniffed the volcano and sneezed.

"Is *that* your science fair project?" Luke shook his head. "A volcano? Everybody makes volcanoes!"

Matt suddenly pictured a room full of volcanoes. Allison's would be the biggest. He shook his head to make the picture go away. "Eddie said he had a plan to make this better than any volcano in the history of the world!"

Luke snorted. "And you believe him? Gosh, what a doofus." Luke picked up Mittens and went back inside.

Matt turned back to his project. It no longer looked quite so shiny.

On Monday Matt got up to go to school. Then he went right back to bed. His head felt hot. His muscles ached. His tummy hurt.

"Mo-o-o-m," he called.

Mom came in. Her hand felt cool on his

hot forehead. Her shiny black hair swung down. The scent of her shampoo drifted over him.

"Sorry, kiddo," said Mom. "Looks like you have a bug. You'll have to stay home from school today."

Matt pictured himself in bed with a cartoony-looking insect. Something big, with orange and purple stripes. Maybe with little bitty wings and bobbing antennae. He'd draw a picture of it later.

But now, Matt felt too sick to draw. He ran to the bathroom and made it just in time. He spent the rest of the day sleeping or sitting on the toilet. Mittens snored gently on the end of his bed.

On Tuesday he felt well enough to sit up. Mom brought him ginger ale and soda crackers. She sat on the end of the bed while he sipped.

"You get the BRAT diet today," she said, smoothing back the hair from Matt's forehead.

Matt looked puzzled. "The BRAT diet?" asked Matt. "What's that?"

"Bananas, rice, applesauce, and toast," said Mom. "Plenty of fluids and no dairy." Mom was a nurse. She knew about things like that.

"If your tummy settles down, you can go to school tomorrow," said Mom. "I called Eddie. He'll drop off your homework after school today."

Matt read books. He watched soap operas on TV. He played video games. He didn't have to go to the bathroom as much. After lunch he took a nap.

When he woke up, he felt better. The rumblings in his tummy were over. He sat up in bed. He drew a picture of Frankenstein skateboarding. Matt gave the monster a big scar across his face. He was just sketching in thin lines for stitches when he heard the roar of the school bus outside.

He ran to his window and looked out.

Eddie's house was just across the street. It was so close that they often signaled to each other with flashlights at night— when they were supposed to be asleep.

Matt saw Mittens sitting on top of Eddie's roof. She was basking in the sunshine. She liked to sit up there. Out of reach of Lorrie, Eddie's little sister. Lorrie just loved Mittens. But Mittens did not love Lorrie.

The bus doors screeched open. Lorrie jumped down the bus stairs. She was a tiny kindergartner—as thin as a whistle, her pale blonde hair pulled back in a ponytail. Matt thought she looked like a little mouse. But she was stronger than she looked. Matt had often seen her swinging on the monkey bars at school.

Eddie got off next. He turned to yell at someone on the bus. He went inside his house. After a while, he came out with his skateboard. He coasted over to Matt's house.

Matt smiled. Trust Eddie. Even though their houses were so close you could practically step from one porch to the other, Eddie had to ride his skateboard.

Downstairs, Matt heard the doorbell ring. A few minutes later, Mom came up with a glass of ginger ale and some soda crackers. "Eddie brought your homework," she said. "I told him you could probably go to school tomorrow."

Satisfied, Matt went back to bed. He was worn out. He shoved his crayons onto the floor and went to sleep.

Chapter Five

Don't Miss the Bus

The next morning Matt woke up early. Mom came in while he was still in bed. She took his temperature.

"No fever," she said, sliding the thermometer back inside the cardboard tube. "You can go to school today."

Matt gave her a high five. "Yes!" he said. "Is the volcano dry? I want to take it to school to show Eddie."

Mom laughed. "Yes, it's dry. I checked it last night. But, honey," she added, "why take it to school? It would be easier to show it to him here. After school."

Matt shook his head. He could never wait that long.

Mom smiled. "Okay. But you'd better get going if you're going to catch the bus," she said.

Mom kissed him good-bye. She left for her job at the hospital.

Matt ate cornflakes with brown sugar and milk. His tummy felt fine. Mom had left his lunch sack ready for him on the counter. He went upstairs to wash his face and put on his shoes.

But he couldn't find his left shoe. He hopped around his room on one foot looking for it. Mittens helped him look. She went under his desk. She found a piece of scrunched up paper. She batted it out.

"Hustle, Matthew!" called Dad. "The bus is here!"

Matt finally found his shoe under the bed. He also found his baseball and three skateboard magazines.

"I wondered where those were," he said to Mittens. By the time he got his shoe on, the bus was gone.

Dad had to drop Matt at school on his way to work. It turned out to be a good thing, because the volcano would not fit in Matt's backpack. He put it in a Big-Mart plastic sack. He held it on his lap while Dad drove.

Matt liked riding with Dad. The car smelled like old french fries, but Dad smelled good. He wore a suit and tie for his job at the bank.

"All excited about the science fair, Matt?" asked Dad. He pulled out of the driveway.

"Only a week to go," said Matt. "I wish Eddie would tell me what he's planning. I sure hope it's good enough to win!"

"Your mom and I are really proud of you for entering," Dad said. "But don't get too caught up in winning. The important thing is that you and Eddie showed initiative by entering and actually finished your project."

Matt sat back. He zipped up his sweat-shirt. He smiled at Dad. But he wasn't convinced. He knew what was important. A new skateboard. *That* was important.

A few minutes later, Dad pulled into the school driveway. Matt was early. The buses weren't even there yet.

Matt kissed Dad good-bye.

"See you at dinner, sport," said Dad. "Good luck with the volcano."

Chapter Six

Traitor

Matt waved good-bye as Dad drove away. He slung his backpack over his shoulder. He grabbed the sack with the volcano. It was light but bulky.

He went to wait outside Mrs. Gonzales's door. He was first in line.

The duty teacher blew the whistle. Kids scattered across the playground, chasing balls, gathering up jackets, sweaters, and backpacks.

One by one, the rest of Mrs. Gonzales's class skidded into line: Brittany, Jasmine,

Michael Sanchez, Michael Black, Allison, and the others.

Eddie was last. He ran up behind Allison and slid. She jumped out of the way just in time.

"Hey, Diarrhea Boy is back!" yelled Brittany. There was a small gasp. Then someone snickered. Matt looked around. Brittany couldn't be talking about him, could she?

"Hey, Matt-a-rhea!" called Michael Black.

Jasmine giggled.

"That's not very nice," sniffed Allison.

They *were* talking about him. Matt stared at the kids, horrified. Heat flooded his face. He glanced at Eddie. Eddie didn't meet his eyes.

Just then, Mrs. Gonzales opened the door. "Good morning, class!" she said in her cheery voice. Everyone stopped laughing and lined up.

"Good morning, Mrs. Gonzales," sang

Brittany in a goody-goody voice. But as soon as Mrs. Gonzales turned her back, Brittany smirked at Matt.

Matt liked Mrs. Gonzales. Even though she was old, Matt thought she was the nicest third-grade teacher in the school. With her dimples and curly gray hair, he usually thought she looked like a friendly squirrel.

But today he didn't care if she looked like Dracula.

All morning long he heard whispers and snickers. They are laughing at me, he thought. What was going on?

He kept his head down, trying to concentrate on his math work sheet. Trying not to let the lump in his throat leak out in tears.

Matt tried to catch Eddie's eye. But Eddie kept his head down, too. The tips of his ears were red. Why was Eddie embarrassed? They weren't laughing at *him*! Matt turned back to his work.

The hands of the clock crept slowly around the dial. Finally, it was time for lunch. Maybe the kids would forget all about teasing him.

Matt got his lunch sack out of his backpack.

Brittany pushed past him on her way to the cafeteria. "What are you having for lunch, Matt-a-rhea?" she asked in a loud voice. "Prunes?"

Michael Black and Victor howled with laughter. Michael Sanchez clutched his sides, pretending it hurt to laugh.

Matt clenched his hands but didn't say anything.

Soon the classroom was empty except for Eddie and Matt. "Listen," said Eddie. "Ignore those guys. Let's go eat."

They sat side by side in the cafeteria.

Matt opened his lunch sack but didn't pull anything out. He stared into it for a bit. Then he scrunched it back up.

He looked at Eddie. "What's going on, Eddie?" he whispered.

Eddie shook his head. "It wasn't me. I swear, Matt. Cross my heart and hope to die. It wasn't me. Only . . ." He paused.

"Only what?" Matt asked.

"Only maybe I did say something, just by accident. Only I didn't mean to." Eddie pushed his glasses back up on his nose. The round lenses made his eyes look big.

"You were the only one my mom told," said Matt, still in that strange, quiet voice.

Just then, Allison slid into the seat across from them. She set down her tray.

"Hi, Matt," she said. "Eddie told the class you were sick. I hope you're feeling better now."

She unrolled her napkin neatly. She set out her fork and spoon. She took a dainty bite of mashed potatoes and gravy. Then she paused.

"Of course, what Eddie *actually* said was really gross. He used a vulgar word. Definitely not a school word. Said it in front of Mrs. Gonzales and the whole class, too."

Matt's mouth opened in an *O*. He looked at Eddie. Eddie didn't meet his eyes. Eddie drew with the tip of his spoon in his mashed potatoes.

"You told everybody I had diarrhea?" asked Matt in a hushed voice. He couldn't believe it.

Finally, Eddie looked up. He grinned. "Come on. Lighten up! It's funny!"

Matt's face blazed. His eyes felt like hot lava as he glared at Eddie.

"Traitor!" he shouted. He banged his fist down on the table, making Eddie's tray jump. "YOU TOLD THE WHOLE CLASS I HAD DIARRHEA?" he yelled. "WHAT KIND OF A FRIEND ARE YOU?"

Matt didn't notice the shocked hush in the cafeteria. He didn't hear the ripple of laughter that followed. He was too busy storming out of the cafeteria, his lunch bag crumpled in his fist.

Matt didn't know how he found himself back in Mrs. Gonzales's classroom. He was so angry, his head buzzed like a beehive.

The classroom was empty. Matt threw his uneaten lunch into his backpack. His volcano was in a sack on the floor.

His hands shook so hard, he could hardly get it out of the sack.

"Some partner," he muttered. "I'll show him."

He grabbed the big shears from Mrs. Gonzales's desk. There was a dull ringing in his ears. The scissors sliced right through the papier-mâché. He cut the volcano into two ragged halves.

Then he stomped back to Mrs. Gonzales's desk. He ripped off a big piece of masking tape. He stuck it on half of the volcano. He grabbed a permanent marker. He scrawled "MATT'S HALF" in wobbly black letters across the tape.

"What's going on?"

Matt turned around. Eddie was in the doorway, Allison right behind him.

"You really stink, you know that?" said Matt. He picked up his broken half of the volcano. "I'm taking my half home. I don't care what you do with yours. As far as I'm concerned, we aren't partners anymore! Ever! We're not even friends!"

He kicked Eddie's half of the volcano across the floor. Eddie watched. He didn't say a word.

Allison shook her head. "You guys are like baking soda and vinegar," she said in a snippy voice. "Put you together and FIZZZZZT!"

Chapter Seven
Waiting to Explode

Finally, the bell rang. School was out. Matt's face hurt from scowling all afternoon, but it was the only way he could keep from crying.

He ignored Eddie on the bus. He sat in the very back. He put his backpack, and his half of the volcano, on the seat next to him. That way, Eddie couldn't sit next to him.

When the bus stopped, he stomped down the aisle. He jumped down the bus steps. "Matt!" Eddie called.

Matt ignored him and ran home.

Luke was already home. Matt could hear music thumping from his room.

Matt dropped his half of the volcano by the front door. He ran into the kitchen, skidding a little on the floor. He flung open the fridge. There was only one carton of yogurt left. Strawberry-banana. Figured. He hated strawberry-banana.

He slammed the door shut. He knew he wasn't supposed to. What did he care? Life was ruined.

Mittens came into the kitchen when she heard the refrigerator door. She rubbed up against Matt's leg. She arched her back and meowed.

Usually, Matt fed her and scratched her back while she ate. But today, he just stepped over her and pretended he didn't know she was hungry.

Luke tromped into the kitchen. Matt could hear his big feet coming all the way downstairs. Luke held an empty carton of yogurt. Cherry. Matt's favorite. Luke had eaten the last cherry yogurt. Figured!

"How was school, little bro?" Luke asked. He had a yogurt mustache on his upper lip.

"Okay," Matt said. No way he was telling Luke what really happened.

Just then the doorbell rang. Matt raced down the hall and flung the front door open.

Eddie stood on the steps. He looked just the same. Good old crazy Eddie, grinning his happy grin. His glasses slid down his nose.

Matt's face hardened. "What do you want?" he asked.

"Want to skateboard?" asked Eddie. "We can take turns on mine."

Matt seethed. Eddie wasn't even trying to apologize. Figured! He slammed the door in Eddie's face. He felt like a volcano himself, just waiting to explode.

He went into the kitchen to feed Mittens. His foot kicked Mitten's water bowl. Water slopped out. He grabbed a paper towel and mopped it up. He scolded poor Mittens as if she'd spilled her own water.

Matt spent the afternoon slumped on the living-room couch. Staring out the window. The October rains had started. Across the street, Matt saw Eddie in his yellow slicker, skateboarding in the drizzle.

With a heavy sigh, Matt stomped upstairs. He'd draw a picture. That would make him feel better.

But it didn't make him feel better. His favorite red crayon snapped. Then, when he tried to sharpen his black crayon, it broke off in the sharpener. He dug at it with a paper clip, but he couldn't get it out. Now he didn't even have a sharpener anymore! He crumpled up his piece of paper. He threw it on the floor. It was all Eddie's fault.

He swept a herd of plastic dinosaurs off his desk. He grabbed a pencil and a fresh sheet of paper. He began to draw tornadoes, lightning bolts, and hurricanes. It looked like scribbling, and it felt good.

Chapter Eight

Some Friend

The next day at school was the most awful day of Matt's life.

"Prunes," whispered Brittany every time Matt went by. That meant both Michaels and Victor had to tease him, too. They always did everything Brittany did.

At recess Eddie played football with the Michaels. That traitor! Matt stood by the tetherball pole with his hands jammed into his pockets. Clouds as black as Matt's mood loomed overhead.

Allison came up behind him. "What are you going to do about the science fair?" she asked. "Jasmine and I are making a pinhole camera. That's very hard to do. It will impress the judges. We're sure to win first place."

She flipped back her long hair. She peered at him with her pale eyes as if he was a science experiment. He made a face, but she didn't go away.

"I guess you'll have to drop out, huh?" she said. "The science fair is tomorrow, you know. You don't have time to get a new partner. You don't have time to make a new project."

The football bounced across the field and landed at Matt's feet. The two Michaels ran over.

"Hey! Wait till you see our project," said Michael S. "It's a model of the solar system. With glow-in-the-dark paint and glitter."

"Yeah, that prize money is as good as

ours." Michael B. grabbed the football and tucked it under his arm. "Too bad you have to drop out." He laughed, and the two Michaels ran off.

Matt could almost see his new skateboard sprout wings and fly away.

He didn't care. He stood in the cold wind, feeling sorry for himself and glaring at Eddie. Eddie didn't notice. He kept right on running and grinning like the traitor he was.

Some friends weren't worth keeping.

At lunch Eddie dropped his lunch tray with a bang and slid next to Matt. Just like nothing had happened. What nerve!

"Look!" said Eddie. "Watch this!"

He took two green beans and stuck them in his nostrils. He took two dried apricot slices and put them over his eyes. He stuck two carrot sticks under his upper lip. They hung down like fangs.

"Monster face!" he yelled.

It was just like Eddie to try to make up,

thought Matt furiously. Act silly—and not one word of apology. In the old days, Matt would have laughed and they'd be friends again. But not today. Today, Matt didn't say a word. He just glared at Eddie.

"Come on! Lighten up!" said Eddie. But his voice lacked the old Eddie self-confidence.

Eddie slowly took the food off his face. He looked at Matt.

When he spoke, Matt hardly recognized his former friend's voice, it was so quiet.

"See," said Eddie. "Mrs. Gonzales just told me I'm flunking science. I need those fifty points she'll give me for a science fair project. We can't drop out now."

Eddie paused. He pushed his glasses up. "Because if I flunk science, what am I going to tell my dad?"

Matt considered. Should he take Eddie back? It would be awful if he flunked science.

But then Allison turned around. She flipped her hair back.

"Can't you see that Matt doesn't want you for a friend?" she said. "After what you did? He's got more sense than to make up with a crazy kid like you."

Eddie's face fell. He swept up all the food back onto his tray and dumped it in the trash. Matt watched as Eddie jammed his hands into the pockets of his jeans and walked out of the cafeteria.

Chapter Nine

Help!

After school Matt rode the bus home. He looked out the window. Rain clouds gathered overhead.

That traitor, Eddie, hadn't even tried to sit next to him. He flopped into a seat several rows in front of Matt.

Matt stared at the back of Eddie's head all the way home. The stupid way his hair stuck up on top. His stupid skinny neck and sticking-out ears.

It isn't my fault if Eddie flunks science, he thought. Eddie and his stupid ideas.

Maybe this would teach him to be more careful about saying things next time.

Matt looked out the window. Raindrops streaked down the glass. Maybe Eddie was a loose cannon like Dad said.

Matt remembered the time Eddie had tried to make fireworks. He almost set the garage on fire.

He remembered the time Eddie tried to build a time machine out of Luke's bicycle. Matt started to grin. Boy was Luke mad when they crashed his bike on Dead Man's Hill! They'd been grounded for a week. Matt's smile faded.

He didn't have to worry about Eddie's crazy ideas anymore. He wasn't ever going to play with that traitor again! Matt pressed his nose against the bus window and watched the rain drip down the glass. He liked the old days better.

When he got home, Matt ran up the steps to his house. He dropped his backpack on the floor. He went into the kitchen and got a banana. While he was peeling it, the doorbell rang.

Lorrie stood on the steps, her blonde ponytail coming undone. "Can I play with Mittens?" she asked.

Matt felt mean. "No!" he yelled. He knew it wasn't Lorrie's fault, but he didn't want anything to do with any Hamptons, ever.

He slammed the door and ran upstairs to draw.

It was almost dark when Mom got home.

"Matt," she called. "I'm home!" He ran downstairs.

Mom gave him a kiss. "How was school?"

"Okay." Matt didn't look at her. But for once, Mom didn't notice his mood. She was busy digging around in the kitchen cupboard. "Oh no, we're out of tuna," she said. "I'll have to run to the grocery store.

"Please take the garbage out, honey," Mom added. "Tomorrow is trash day. And knock on Luke's door and tell him to set the table. I'll be right back." She grabbed her purse and went out the garage door.

Matt went outside to set the garbage can by the curb, so the truck would pick it up in the morning. He shivered in the cold air. The sky was turning pale. Bare trees stuck up like bony fingers, black and threatening. Only a few weeks until Halloween.

"Matt!"

Matt looked around. No one was there.

"Matt!" A thin voice sliced the air. "Help! Up here!"

Matt looked toward Eddie's house. Lorrie was on top of her roof. She clung to the chimney.

"Lorrie? What are you doing up there?"

Lorrie's face was white. "I'm stuck!" she yelled. "Get me down!"

"But how did you get up there?"

"I wanted to play with Mittens!"

Mittens! Matt looked down. Mittens wove in and out of his legs, rubbing against them.

"You said I couldn't play with him in But I saw her on the roof." ...led him in

Matt felt like so...is fault Lorrie was the stomach. It on the roof

"Hurry, Matt! I'm scared!" Lorrie started to cry.

Chapter Ten

Hang On

"Hang on!" Matt called. He ran up the steps to Eddie's front door. He rang the bell and pounded.

Eddie opened the door. He frowned when he saw Matt standing there. "What do you want?" Matt grabbed his arm.

"It's Lorrie! She's stuck on the roof!" Matt hauled him down to the sidewalk. Matt pointed to the roof.

"Lorrie? What the heck are you doing up there?" Eddie yelled. "You'd better get down right now!"

Lorrie sat down, still clinging to the chimney. "I can't! I'm scared!" she yelled, her voice cracking.

"Shouldn't we get your mom?" Matt asked Eddie.

"Mom's not home yet," Eddie told Matt. "Only Cinda, our baby-sitter. She's on her cell phone talking to her dumb old boyfriend, again. She's no help."

Lorrie began to cry harder. "I'm cold!"

Matt and Eddie stared at each other. What should they do?

"Should we call 911?" asked Matt.

Eddie shook his head. "I think 911 is only if you're bleeding or dying or something."

"Should we wait until my dad gets home?" Matt shaded his eyes to look up at Lorrie.

"No!" yelled Lorrie. "Don't wait! I'm scared! Get me down now!"

Eddie walked over to the house. "She

got up there by herself somehow. I think we can get her down."

"Where's your ladder?" asked Matt.

Eddie shook his head. "No ladder."

"There's a ladder at my house," said Matt. "Let's go!"

"Hang on, Lorrie!" shouted Eddie. "We'll rescue you!"

The ladder was in the garage. It took both of them to carry it. They dragged it to Eddie's house.

Matt held the ladder steady while Eddie climbed up. Eddie stood on the top step of the ladder. He held out his hand. "Come on, Lorrie. Give me your hand."

Lorrie peered down at him. "I can't! I'm too scared!"

Eddie sighed. "How am I going to help you, then? You have to give me your hand."

Matt remembered once when he was stuck in a tree. He was afraid to come down. The ground looked so far away. Dad had helped him get down. Now he remembered what to do.

"Turn around, Lorrie!" he called. "Kneel with your back to Eddie, so you can't see the ground. Eddie, set her foot on the ladder."

"I get it!" said Eddie.

Eddie gently guided Lorrie's foot to the ladder's top step.

"Feel the step?" he asked. His voice was soft. "I'm holding you. You're okay, Lorrie. You're safe."

Lorrie nodded. She backed down the ladder. Eddie put his arm around her.

Matt held the ladder steady as Eddie guided his little sister down. When they were on the ground, Lorrie threw her arms around Matt and Eddie.

"You guys saved my life!" She squeezed them so tightly they were almost nose to nose.

Matt looked at Eddie. Eddie looked

down. Matt couldn't tell what he was thinking.

Lorrie dropped her arms. She wiped her eyes with the tail of her T-shirt. "I'm shaking! And I'm cold. And hungry. I'm going inside. Cinda will make me hot chocolate."

Eddie caught her arm. "Just a minute. How did you get up there, anyway?"

Lorrie rubbed her nose on the back of her hand. Her ponytail had come undone. "I wanted to play with Mittens. At first, I couldn't figure out how to get up there. Then Cinda's mom drove Cinda over here to baby-sit. You know that black Jeep they have? It's pretty tall."

Lorrie continued. "I stood on the bumper and climbed up. Then I pulled myself up to our roof. It was just like the monkey bars at school. But when I was on the roof, Cinda's mom drove away."

Lorrie laughed. She wasn't scared anymore. "It's kind of funny! She drove away. And there I was—trapped on the roof!"

"Mittens wasn't stuck," said Matt. "She likes to sleep up there." Matt leaned down to pet her. Mittens purred.

"I know that now," said Lorrie. "'Cause after Cinda's mom drove away, Mittens climbed down that rose thingy."

She pointed to the trellis. "But I'm too heavy for that. I was scared. And then you guys came."

She gave them another grin and ran inside.

Eddie turned to Matt. "Thanks," he said. "I'll help you take the ladder back."

He pulled the ladder down. Matt grabbed the other end.

"You know that bad thing I said?" Eddie turned around. His gray eyes were serious for once.

"Yeah?" Matt grunted under the weight of the ladder.

"I'm sorry." Eddie picked up the ladder. "It wasn't funny. I shouldn't have said it."

Matt looked at him in surprise. Crazy Eddie, apologizing!

"S'okay," said Matt.

"So. You want to be partners again?"

"Yeah." Matt grinned. "I want to be partners again."

Chapter Eleven

Volcano!

Matt and Eddie spent the evening at Matt's house, trying to fix the volcano. They taped it together, but there were big, ragged holes. Part of it was torn. It looked terrible.

"It's no good," said Eddie, shaking his head. He rocked back on his heels. "This will never work. There just isn't time to do it over."

Matt had to agree. It looked awful. Now was the time for one of Eddie's great ideas. Matt pictured Eddie with a light-bulb over his head, like a cartoon of some-one having an idea.

"Okay, Eddie. Tell me. What's your great idea?"

Eddie grinned and pushed his glasses up on his nose. Matt breathed a sigh. It was going to be all right. Eddie would save the day.

"See," said Eddie, "I think we should take swim fins and put them on and walk around in the mud by the play-ground at school and leave really cool footprints. Brittany will think it was giant frogs."

Matt stared at Eddie. What they needed was a great idea. An idea worthy of

Orville Wright or Thomas Edison. And all they got was giant frogs! *"That's* it?"

Eddie nodded happily.

Giant frog footprints! That would never win the science fair!

Matt blinked quickly to hide his disappointment. He scratched Mittens under the chin. It was up to him. His mind went around in circles. Volcanoes. Hot lava. Thomas Edison. Lightbulbs.

Suddenly, he had it.

"Listen!" said Matt. "I've got the best idea ever!"

They worked until bedtime on Matt's crazy plan.

Friday night was the science fair. After dinner, Matt, Mom, Dad, and Luke drove back to school.

The room shone. Mrs.

Gonzales, her dimples flashing, stood at the door greeting parents as they came in.

Mrs. Hampton was already there with Lorrie. Mom and Dad stopped to talk to her. Matt carried the volcano model in a Big-Mart sack. He searched the room for Eddie.

The noise was unbelievable. The classroom was crowded with parents and kids. Nearly everyone in third grade had entered the fair. Science projects were set up all over the desks, counters, and tables. The room smelled like rotten eggs.

"Hey, Matt!" Eddie waved. Matt quickly wound his way through the crowded room. They pushed their desks together and set up their project.

Eddie put out bottles of vinegar, dishwashing liquid, and red food coloring. Matt got out a box of baking soda and measuring spoons.

Eddie had made a sign, and they taped it to the front of the desk: SEE THE FIERY VOLCANO.

At last, Matt reached into his sack and pulled out the volcano. He couldn't wait to see his brilliant idea again.

Last night Matt had taped red Christmas lights inside the volcano. Now, Matt plugged them in and stepped back to admire it. Red lights flickered through the holes of the torn papier-mâché. The volcano burned with fiery light.

Eddie whistled. "Wow."

Matt glowed with pride.

Matt looked around the room at the other projects. Brittany and Victor had made a display of how plants grew in sunlight and dark. The vines kept falling down. Brittany scrambled to tape them back up.

Matt shook his head. No way that project was going to win.

Michael Sanchez and Michael Black had made a model of the solar system out of different-sized balls. Some of the balls weren't stuck on very well. Jupiter fell off and bounced down the aisle. The two Michaels didn't look too worried, though. Michael Black just laughed as he chased the runaway planet.

There were potato clocks and rock collections and a pet iguana in a tank.

Allison and Jasmine had a very fancy display of a pinhole camera and the pictures they had taken. They'd even typed up a report about it. Matt had to admit it was pretty slick.

It was time to start. Matt and Eddie stood side by side demonstrating the volcano. Eddie poured in the baking soda. Matt added the dishwashing liquid, red food coloring, and vinegar.

FIZZZZZT! The lava foamed up over the top of the crater. It oozed down the slopes.

"Eruption! Run for your lives!" yelled Eddie.

"Ooh, red-hot lava!" said Lorrie when she saw it.

Luke stopped by their table. "Not bad, little bro," he said. "But next time you should use ammonium dichromate!"

"Maybe when we get to middle school," said Matt.

Mrs. Hampton, Mom, and Dad came over. They wanted to see the volcano erupt, too.

"I'm proud of you, sport," said Dad. "You started a project and you finished it. Good job." He reached over and ruffled Matt's hair.

"And the Christmas lights look wonderful," added Mom. "Great touch." She gave him a hug. Matt grinned.

Finally, it was time for the judging. The judges wore badges and carried clipboards. They went around the room, stopping at each project, making notes.

Then the judges called for everyone's attention. Tingles of excitement ran through Matt.

"We'd like to thank everyone for coming," began the tall judge. He announced third place—the iguana, and second place—a remote-control car that ran on a potato battery.

Then the judge paused. "And now, for first place," he said. Matt held his breath. "First place goes to Allison and Jasmine for their excellent pinhole camera project."

Matt swallowed his disappointment. Allison was right, he thought. The pinhole camera had impressed the judges. The girls went up to the front of the room to collect their ribbons and the gift certificate.

On the way back, Allison stopped by Matt and Eddie's volcano.

"Congratulations, Allison," said Matt. "You deserved it."

Allison looked surprised. "You aren't

mad? But now you can't buy your skate-board."

Matt shook his head. "Nah. I'm not mad. Some things are just more impor-tant than winning, you know?"

"Oh, sure," said Allison. She grinned. "I know what you mean. School just wouldn't be the same without Matt and Eddie together again at last."

Eddie turned around. He had painted red food coloring stripes on each cheek, like whiskers. "And we each get fifty points just for entering, so I won't flunk science. And that makes my dad happy. And Matt can use my skateboard anytime he wants."

"And my birthday is just two months away, so if anybody wants to know what to get me . . ." Matt looked at his parents. "Hint, hint!" he said.

The science fair was over. Parents gath-ered up coats and small children. The kids took down their projects. Matt's parents waited for him by the door, talking to Mrs. Gonzales.

Matt got a sponge out of the cupboard. He wiped up the spilled lava. Eddie put caps on the food coloring and dishwashing liquid.

"All out of vinegar," he said, tossing the bottle in the trash. "I guess we did pretty good."

"Got that right," said Matt.

Suddenly, Eddie turned to Matt. "Listen! Do you think you can sleep over at my house tonight? Because when I saw Lorrie on the roof, it gave me a great idea. If we take our blankets and use them like parachutes, do you think we can . . . ?"

Matt stopped listening. That Eddie! That crazy, crazy Eddie!

How to Make a Volcano That Really Erupts

by Matt and Eddie

We did this for our science fair. Mrs. Gonzales said we had to write this report to get our fifty points of extra credit. So here it is. We hope you like it.

We made a model volcano that really erupts, using baking soda, vinegar, dishwashing liquid, and red food coloring. You can make one, too.

First, you need a plastic bottle, like a soft-drink bottle or water bottle, and a big piece of cardboard for the ground. If you want to make it glow, wrap red Christmas lights around the bottle. Use masking tape to tape strips from the mouth of the bottle to the cardboard. Do this all around the bottle so it makes a masking-tape cone.

Next, make flour paste. Mix one cup of warm water and one cup of flour together. Then add four more cups of warm water. Mix it well.

Now you can make papier-mâché by tearing old newspapers into strips and soaking them in the water-and-flour mixture. This is the gooshy part! Do not use the newspaper your dad has not read yet.

Spread the wet paper strips all around on the masking tape. Start at the bottom of the volcano and paste them right over each other, overlapping, all the way to the top. The masking tape will give your volcano nice canyons and valleys. Be sure not to cover the mouth of the plastic bottle. That is your crater. That is where you put the lava. Punch some holes in the papier-mâché so the lights will show.

When the papier-mâché is dry, paint the volcano. We painted ours green for forests and brown for rocks and a little bit of white around the crater for snow.

When the paint is dry, you can make your volcano erupt. First, use a funnel to pour four tablespoons of baking soda into the crater. Then add six drops of dishwashing liquid. Add a few drops of red food coloring.

Now you are ready for the vinegar! Put in two tablespoons, or more if you want to! Now stand back and watch it blow!

Oh, yeah. Be sure to put a newspaper or box underneath the volcano so you don't make a mess.